PENGUIN CLASSICS

THE SONG OF THE LARK

Willa Cather was born in December 1873 in Back Creek Valley, Virginia, the eldest child of Charles and Mary Cather, both descendants of established Virginian families. Her childhood was reportedly happy and well ordered, and is remembered in her late novel *Sapphira and the Slave Girl*. In 1883, the Cathers moved to Webster County, Nebraska, joining members of the family who had settled there earlier. This crucial move, dislocating and dramatic, introduced Cather to a landscape and to ways of life she would memorialize in her famous prairie novels, *O Pioneers!*, *My Ántonia*, and *A Lost Lady*, as well as in parts of *The Song of the Lark*. In the small town of Red Cloud, Nebraska, Cather was a notably energetic, intelligent, and outspoken child, while, as her novels show, the town often seemed to her repressive. In Lincoln, Nebraska, where she attended the state university, she began her journalistic career, writing numerous reviews for the local newspapers. There, too, she published her earliest stories, formulated her idealistic and romantic vision of art, and nurtured her literary ambitions. Those ambitions had to wait for their fulfillment while she earned a living in Pittsburgh as journalist and teacher, and then in New York as an editor for *McClure's Magazine*. With the publication of *O Pioneers!* in 1913, Cather became the dedicated writer of her own dreams, in time achieving recognition for her prairie novels and for rare and unique works such as *The Professor's House*, *Death Comes for the Archbishop*, and *Shadows on the Rock*. She led an ordered life, writing stories, novels, and critical essays, traveling regularly, and maintaining valued friendships, among them with neighbors from her childhood, as well as with famous writers and musicians. She was honored for her writings, receiving the Pulitzer Prize in 1923 for *One of Ours*, a novel about a soldier in World War I. She died at her home in New York in 1947.

Sherrill Harbison is visiting lecturer at Trinity College, Hartford, and an associate of the Five Colleges in Amherst, Massachusetts. She received her B.A. from Oberlin College and her Ph.D. from the University of Massachusetts, Amherst. Her awards include the Aurora Borealis Prize, and grants from the National Endowment for the Humanities, the Fulbright Commission, and the Norwegian Marshall Fund. She has published translations and articles on Willa Cather, William Faulkner, and Sigrid Undset, and she is also the editor of the Penguin Twentieth-Century Classics edition of Undset's novel *Gunnar's Daughter*.